VICTOR
and
CHRISTABEL

by Petra Mathers

Alfred A. Knopf · New York

Vittore Carpaccio's painting *Saint Ursula's Dream* (ca. 1495), which hangs in the Gallerìa Dell'Accadèmia in Venice, was the inspiration for Petra Mathers's *Cousin Christabel on Her Sickbed* (1992), which appears in this book.

THIS IS A BORZOI BOOK PUBLISHED BY ALFRED A. KNOPF, INC.

Copyright © 1993 by Petra Mathers
All rights reserved under International and Pan-American Copyright Conventions. Published in the United States by Alfred A. Knopf, Inc., New York, and simultaneously in Canada by Random House of Canada Limited, Toronto. Distributed by Random House, Inc., New York. Book design by Edward Miller.

Library of Congress Cataloging-in-Publication Data
Mathers, Petra.
    Victor and Christabel / by Petra Mathers.
        p. cm.
    Summary: The shy guard at an art museum falls in love with the sad young woman in a painting that mysteriously appears one day.
    ISBN 0-679-83060-X [trade] — ISBN 0-679-93060-4 [lib. bdg.]
    [1. Painting—Fiction. 2. Magic—Fiction.] I. Title.
PZ7.M42475Vi 1993
[E]—dc20   92-33468

Manufactured in the United States of America
10 9 8 7 6 5 4 3 2 1

Victor

Victor was a guard at a little-known museum off the
beaten track. He was in charge of the Fitzhugh
Simmons Wing. Now and then, some visitors poked
their heads around a pillar, but mostly Victor was alone
with the pictures.

"Rise and shine," he greeted them in the morning.

"Sweet dreams, my dears," he said, closing at night.

Then he walked home, fixed a bite to eat, and went
to bed.

One day, a new picture arrived.

"No idea where this came from," said the museum director.

·COUSIN CHRISTABEL ON HER SICKBED·

Victor read off a little plaque on the frame.

"I have an empty wall," he said quickly.

"She's yours," said the museum director. "Go ahead, hang her."

When COUSIN CHRISTABEL was installed, Victor took a closer look. "What a lovely young woman," he thought, "but so sad, so sad."

·COUSIN CHRISTABEL ON HER SICKBED·

During the next weeks, Victor spent many hours gazing at Cousin Christabel. Her nose was red at the tip; her waxy blue hands clutched the covers.

"Poor dear. Must hurt, whatever she's sick from," thought Victor.

Christabel's room was spacious and filled with large furniture. A fire had died on the hearth, heavy curtains were half-drawn. Even though the sun seemed to be shining, the room looked dark and cold.

But what really puzzled Victor was the broken teacup on the rug. "Must have taken ill quite suddenly, didn't you, dear?" he murmured.

One morning, Victor brought a little night-light. "To keep the goblins away," he said, plugging it into an outlet below the painting.

He began to dread his days off. Even though Christabel's face was fixed in his mind, he missed seeing her. Something about her tugged at his heart. He wanted to bring her hot tea and warm her blue hands in his. He bought flowers—tulips in spring, carnations in summer.

"Bet she's pretty, your young lady," they teased him at the florist's.

"Pretty as a picture," smiled Victor.

He was happy and unhappy all at once. He was in love.

Christabel

Victor and the museum people didn't know where
COUSIN CHRISTABEL ON HER SICKBED came from, but
someone else did. Anatole Fidibus.

He was a magician down on his luck. With no
prospect of work, his last dollar spent, he appeared one
blustery night at his cousin's house.

"Christabel, open up!" he shouted, pounding on
the door.

When she saw him—the wind whipping his cloak,
wet hair glued to his forehead—she tried to shut
him out.

Too late. His foot blocked the way.

"Step aside, you old hearse horse. It's me—Anatole."

Christabel knew her cousin by name only, but rumors had reached her.

"A hot bath and dinner. Now!" he ordered, lugging his bag of tricks upstairs.

Christabel drew his bath, then rummaged through the icebox for his supper. She always did as she was told. Knowing this, she had long ago decided to live alone.

"I don't want him here," she said, sprinkling spices onto a tired slice of meat loaf. "I will tell him he can stay for a few days, no more."

When Anatole entered the kitchen, his bulk seemed to dim the lights.

"I will tell him tomorrow," thought Christabel, and put his plate on the table.

The weeks and months that followed were drudgery. Anatole ran Christabel ragged. She cooked for him, cleaned up after him, and ran his errands. His shopping lists took her to dark parts of town.

skunk juice
liver powder
sulphured slug, sliced
rust cakes

Christabel dragged her heels getting home. "Please be gone," she whispered with each step. But there was Anatole, waiting for her at his window. He'd snatch the bags from her and lock himself in, mumbling and cursing.

Though his spells never worked, they chilled Christabel
to the bone. Then she would fix some tea with honey.

A CUP OF TEA WILL WAKE YOU UP was embroidered on her
tea cozy.

"I feel tired," she'd sigh, and crawl into bed.

One afternoon, when Christabel was down with a cold,
Anatole burst into her room.
"I've got it. This time I've got it," he sputtered.

"Hemlock, Draino, filthy sink,

slimy, rotten, oozing stink,

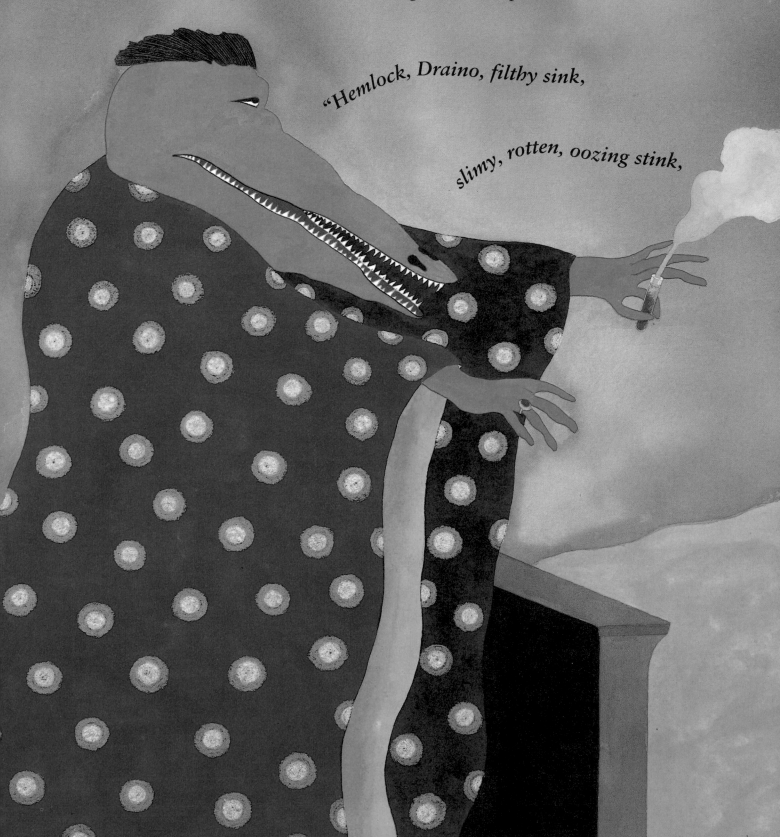

Suddenly Christabel had had enough.
"Out of my house, out of my life!"
she cried, and threw her cup at him.

toes on fire, never blink

from girl to cockroach in a wink."

A CUP OF TEA
WILL WAKE YOU UP

Anatole choked with anger. "You good-for-nothing
mole tail, crawling in and out of bed with your endless
cups of tea, sniffling your life away in your stuffy room.
Stay there, then, red-nosed and bleary-eyed for all the world
to see, like...like a picture in a museum...."

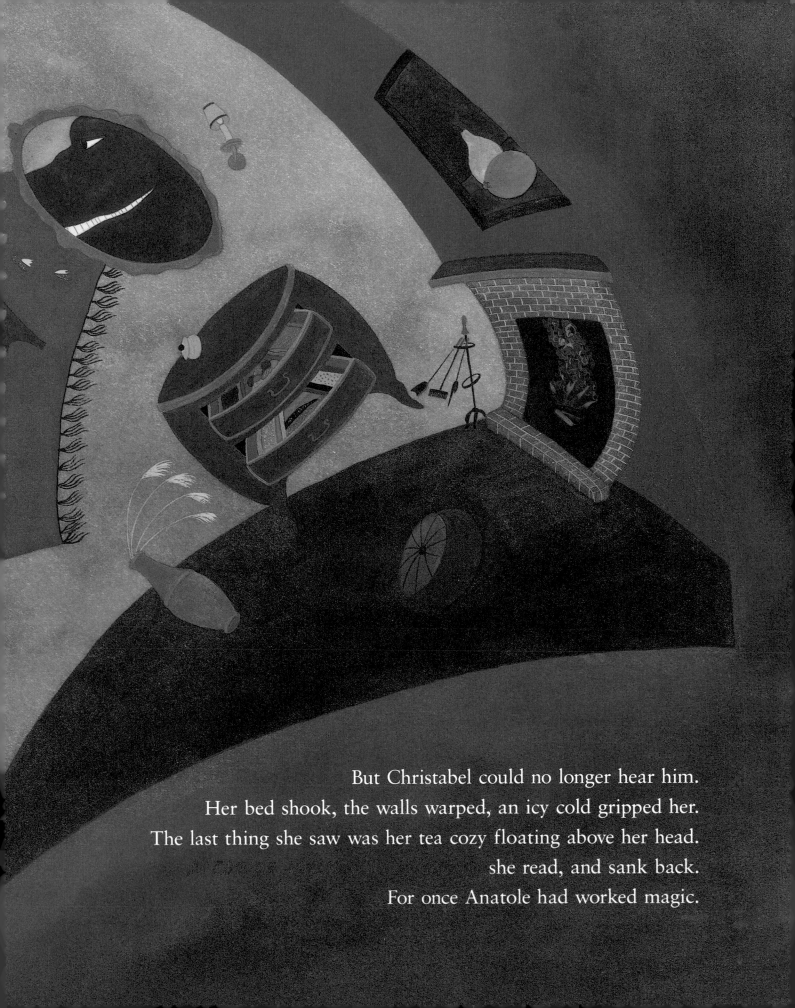

But Christabel could no longer hear him.
Her bed shook, the walls warped, an icy cold gripped her.
The last thing she saw was her tea cozy floating above her head.
she read, and sank back.
For once Anatole had worked magic.

Encouraged by his success, Anatole packed his bags.

"Off you go," he said, hoisting the painting onto his shoulder.

He dropped it off at the nearest museum. "Have a good rest, Cousin," he snickered, and slipped into the night.

Victor and Christabel

Luck had it that Christabel ended up with Victor at the Fitzhugh Simmons Wing.

Few people came to look at her, and Victor was always close by. His gentle voice drifted in and out of her sleep. Her hands felt less icy when he was near. His night-light made the dark less dark, the scent of his flowers sweetened the air around her.

Meanwhile, Victor had grown thin. Love had made him pale and weak. When winter came, he caught a terrible cold.

Since staying home was out of the question, he dragged himself to work. His eyes watering, his nose on fire, he sat in front of his beloved.

Were her hands really less blue, her nose less red?

"I must be out of my mind," he said, and fixed himself some tea with honey.

"I'll just have another look," he thought, and peered at her closely. Steam fogged up his glasses as it rose from his cup.

"Are you feeling better, Chrissy?" he whispered.

"Yes," she said, and flung the covers back.
Victor's heart jumped, his knees gave way.
"Christabel!" he gasped, and fainted.
The spell was broken.

"There now, there, there," murmured Christabel, cradling Victor's head in her lap.

He came to, a thousand questions in his eyes.

"I'll explain later," said Christabel. "We have much time."

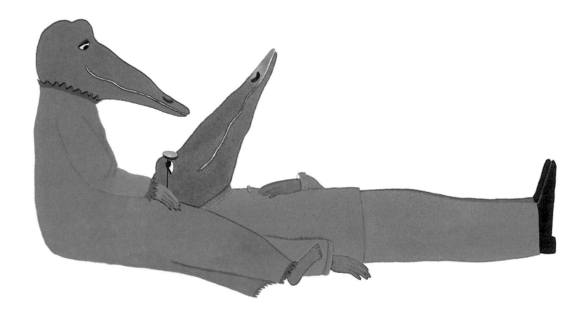

The End